MANDY SWIFTSON

TIMMYS MAGIC BOOK - The Magical Treasure Hunt

First published by Purple Ribbon Publishing 2021

First edition

This book was professionally typeset on Reedsy.
Find out more at reedsy.com

This book is dedicated to some incredibly special people in the life of both the author and the illustrator.

Joey, your love, and imagination keeps me sane (or maybe insane).

Harrison, maybe one day you will listen to this story and know who wrote it.

Oscar and Jasmine Nanny loves you with all her heart.

TO START YOUR ADVENTURE
JUST OPEN YOUR BOOK
TURN THE FIRST PAGE
AND TAKE A LOOK

WHERE WILL IT TAKE YOU?
WHERE WILL YOU BE?
DINOSAURS OR TREASURES?
I CAN'T WAIT TO SEE.

Contents

Foreword

Timmy was first created during the first UK lockdown of 2020. He kept the author Mandy sane and gave her something to work on during this worrying and trying time.

Mandy and Lana first connected after a post on social media during the second UK lockdown of 2020. This quickly became a firm and fast business partnership and also a friendship; and both of them are very excited to see where Timmy and his magic book with all his different adventures takes them.

Preface

Timmy has a wild and magical imagination, he likes to read and he loves adventures, so I decided to combine them all and Timmy's Magic Book series was born. It gave me some much needed light relief during the first national lockdown in the UK during the Covid 19 pandemic. At the same time as writing the first 9 in this series I was also writing "The Mistake" - which is a harrowing true life account of domestic violence and survival. So Timmy's Magic Book allowed me to write something fun and light as well.

Acknowledgement

Thank you to all the little Beta readers who gave us feedback on Timmy and his first adventure.

Thank you to both our families for the love and support we have received during the process of bringing Timmy to life for everyone to enjoy.

Mandy would like to give Lana a special thanks for taking her written ideas and putting the love and life into them,

And you the reader, Thank you for choosing to enjoy Timmy's first adventure with him and us.

TIMMY'S MAGIC BOOK- THE MAGICAL TREASURE HUNT

TO START YOUR ADVENTURE
JUST OPEN YOUR BOOK
TURN THE FIRST PAGE
AND TAKE A LOOK

WHERE WILL IT TAKE YOU?
WHERE WILL YOU BE?
DINOSAURS OR TREASURES?
I CAN'T WAIT TO SEE.

MAGICAL
TREASURE
HUNT

Timmy opened his magic book, he looked inside wondering what fun he would have today. He closed his eyes and ***whoosh*** the magic took him to a faraway place.

When Timmy opened his eyes again, he looked around him in amazement.

He was on a magical island; he knew straight away it was an incredibly special place because all he could see were bright colours and patterns everywhere.

The trees had blue leaves on them.

The sand he was stood on was purple.

The sea to the side of him was orange.

The sky above him was green.

And the clouds, wow the clouds were every colour going. There were clouds with spots on them, there were clouds with stripes on them, there were yellow clouds and red clouds, there were even clouds that were purple with green spots on them. They were Timmy's favourite ones.

As Timmy was smiling in wonder at this amazing place an envelope fluttered down from the sky and landed at his feet.

He bent down and picked it up, it had his name on it so he opened it.

X marks the spot, so find the x
and the treasure you will get.
To find the X just follow the clues,
The clue number one is under the net.

Wow a treasure hunt, Timmy loved treasure hunts, like at Easter when the Easter bunny came, and he had to find the eggs. Timmy was so excited, and he looked around to see if he could see any sort of net.

He spotted a fishing net not too far away; it was one of those big nets that the fishermen use when they go out to sea.

He ran to it straight away eager to start his treasure hunt.

As he got to the net, he saw a ……………

Well Timmy didn't know what it was because he had never seen anything like it before.

He thought it might have been a lizard but it had way too many legs for a lizard.

"Hello" Timmy said. He wasn't at all scared because he knew his magical adventures were always fun and safe not scary and dangerous.

"Who are you? What are you? I have never seen anything like you before. Are you a lizard? I thought you were a lizard at first, but you have a lot of legs to be a lizard."

Timmy talked a lot. His mum and teacher had both said so.

"Crocapus" the creature answered.

"Croa……. what?" asked Timmy

"CROC. A. PUS." He said breaking it down, "you know like my Dad is a crocodile and my Mum is an octopus. Ta-da I am Crocapus" Crocapus answered.

"So, if that is what you are what is your name? My name is Timmy, and I am on a magical adventure, my magic book brought me here for a treasure hunt."

"I am Crocapus and I am a Crocapus, you will only see anyone like me on a magical island, that is why you have never seen anyone like me before."

"Well, this is a VERY magical island, and I am pleased to meet you Crocapus.

My envelope said I would find my clue number one in a net. Do you know where it is please?" Timmy was bouncing up and down in excitement of his treasure hunt.

"Would this be what you are looking for Timmy?" Crocapus asked as he produced an envelope that said 'Number 1'on it.

"Yes, yes, yes" said Timmy.

Crocapus opened the envelope.

"Clue number 1" he began reading.

"To find clue number two,
I have some instructions for you.
Take 4 steps forward.
Then 2 steps back
Take 3 steps left and then find something black!"

Crocapus handed the clue to Timmy when he had finished.

"Something black? Wow that will be hard in all this colour" Timmy said to …………….

No-one. Crocapus had disappeared.

"Crocapus? Crocapus where are you? Where did you go?" Timmy shouted.

"Oh, never mind" Timmy said "I have treasure to find."

Timmy followed his instructions,

"One, two, three, four steps forward. One, two steps back, one, two, three steps left and……"

There in front of Timmy was another strange creature. This wasn't a Crocapus, this was a, a, a something.

"Hello, my name is Timmy, and I am on a magical treasure hunt. What's your name? I met Crocapus but he has disappeared. But I don't think you have a Crocodile for a Dad and an Octopus for a Mum, do you?" Timmy rambled away excitedly.

"No, I don't" the creature asked. "Crocapus is a nice chap but watch out for his brother, he is not so nice."

"Crocapus has a brother! Wow that is so cool, I want a brother but it's just me. My mum says if I had a brother, he wouldn't be able to get a word in edgeways as I talk enough for 4 brothers. I don't know what she means by that, do you know what she means by that? Oh, you still didn't tell me your name".

"Elequar" he answered "and no I have no idea what your mum could mean" he chuckled.

"Elgar" Timmy fumbled around the name,

"No Timmy, try again EL - E - QUAR as in an Elephant and a Jaguar together makes Elequar.

"Elequar, oh I get it now. Elequar my clue said I have to find something black, but I can't see anything black with all these colours, do you know where there is something black?" Timmy answered very quickly, barely even taking a breath.

"Here you go Timmy, you can have this black rock because we don't like things of dark colours on this island"

"Thank-You, Thank-You so much Elequar" Timmy answered as he turned the rock over, finding another envelope this with 'number 2' on it.

"Elequar look! I have found another clue; do you want to read it to me? I mean you don't have to I can read it myself"

"That is fine Timmy, I will read it" Elequar smiled as he took the clue from Timmy.

"Clue number 2

To find clue number 3
Open your eyes and look for the tree.
Walk to the front!
And then around the back
Look to the right!
And find me a sack."

"A tree, back and a sack" got it Timmy said as he fist pumped the air.

"Elequar, do you want to come on my treasure hunt with me? It's so much fun."

"Thank-You Timmy but no, I have got to go I'm afraid. Here is your clue, have fun, Goodbye" Elequar said and ***poof*** he too disappeared.

"Oh well at least he said goodbye" said Timmy before turning his attention back to the clue.

"Look for tree" Timmy said out loud, then turned to see if he could spot one. He could it was just a bit away from him. Timmy ran to it. He stood in front of it, then went around the back and there he found another unusual creature. Timmy stood with his mouth open, looking from side to side trying to decide what it was.

"Hello young Timmy, I have been expecting you" the creature said.

"Hello, have you? How do you know my name? Crocapus and Elequar didn't know me, I had to tell them. So how do you know? Are you magic?" Timmy's words fell from his mouth very quickly causing the creature to laugh.

"So, you have already met Crocapus then, he is a nice friendly chap, so is Elequar. As for how I know your name Timmy, we all know your name, I just got in there before you told me. This is after all YOUR magical treasure hunt Timmy."

"Really you all know my name, that is soooooooooooooo cool. My Mum says I am not allowed to talk to strangers, but I don't think that counts here does it?"

"No Timmy you are quite safe here on your magical treasure hunt, but make sure you listen to your mum at other times. Now my name is Porcubee and I believe you may be looking for this?" Porcubee asked holding a sack out to Timmy.

"Yes, that is what my clue said find me a sack Thank-You Porcubee."

Timmy took the sack.

"Porcubee?" Timmy asked.

"Yes Timmy"

"Crocapus said his Dad was a Crocodile and his Mum an Octopus. Elequar said his name was part Elephant and part Jaguar, what about your name?"

"My Mum is a Porcupine, and my Dad is a Bumblebee, so I am Porcubee."

"Everyone has really cool names here. My name is boring". Timmy said sadly.

"No-one has a boring name Timmy; people just have different names that is all. You think your name is boring, but I think your name is perfect for you. You think my name is cool, but I think it is stupid, we all have things that are seen one way for one and another way for someone else. Now then what is in the sack?" Porcubee answered trying to make Timmy happy again.

"Oh yeah. I bet it's another clue" Timmy cheered up instantly as he looked in the sack.

This time the envelope said 'number 3' on it.

"Porcubee please can I read this one?"

"Of course, you can"

"Clue number 3

To find clue number 4
Look around for an Apple core!
Back to the tree
And look around there.
But don't look on the floor,
Look up in the air."

Timmy looked back at Porcubee,

"I wonder what the treasure will be Porcubee, what do you think it could be? I think it might be some sweets, or maybe a toy, or something to dress up in, or a book. I do hope it's not gold cos that would be boring, unless it is chocolate gold like Santa Claus puts in your stocking, chocolate gold would not be boring because chocolate gold is yummy!"

3

Timmy once again rambled on. The more time he spent on the magical islan. the more the creatures could see what his Mum and Teacher meant about talking a lot.

"I don't know Timmy. But surely part of the excitement is the not knowing what the treasure will be" Porcubee answered laughing.

"Yeah, I guess so"

"So how about you get to locating that Apple core then?"

"Yeah, I will do thanks Porcubee, bye" Timmy said as he ran off leaving Porcubee laughing.

It was very odd because while he had been talking to Porcubee the tree had disappeared. Timmy ran around for a few minutes till he located a tree that he thought was an Apple tree, only when he got closer, he realised it wasn't like any other Apple tree he had ever seen before. (But then being on a magical island in the middle of a magical treasure hunt, having been sent here by a magical book, why would it be?)

You see instead of big fat juicy apples hanging from the tree there were just the cores.

It looked like someone had been and eaten the Apple while it was still hanging, but Timmy knew that wasn't what had happened because there were some tiny ones that looked like they were still growing.

Timmy looked up in the air as the clue had told him to when a core fell from the tree and bounced off Timmy's shoulder onto the floor.

"Sorry about that" said a voice from above "it just kind of slipped, I wasn't trying to hurt you."

"That's ok. I needed to find a way to get one down anyway" Timmy answered.

He bent down and picked up the core and there under it was his next envelope with 'number 4' on it.

"You won't tell anyone I dropped a core on you, will you? I always get into bother cos I am always doing clumsy things I don't mean too it's just what seems to happen Then someone always tells on me and then I get the same talking to be careful watch what you are doing and so on and so on and so on, I mean I don't try to do these thing they just happen. Do you know what I mean Timmy?"

Timmy was almost certain he had never heard someone talk so much without taking a breath.

"Wow. I thought I talked a lot" Timmy laughed "that was really cool though you like talk really quickly and hardly take a breath."

"Yeah, that's the other thing with me, I talk a lot. My mum says it is a good job I only have one brother because I talk enough for 3 or 4 brothers".

"My mum says that about me too, but I don't have any brothers, you are so lucky."

"My brother is ok, not like Crocapus' brother he is grumpy and mean, have you met him yet?"

"Have I met WHO yet? Crocapus? Your brother? Or Crocapus' brother?" Timmy asked scratching his head confused.

"Ha, ha, ha, sorry who have you met so far" the creature came down from the tree.

"Let me see Crocapus gave me the net with clue number 1" Timmy counted them off on his fingers.

"Elequar gave me the rock with clue 2, Porcubee gave me the sack with clue 3 and now you have given me the core with clue 4."

"Well then you haven't met Crocapus' brother yet then, but you have met mine. My brother is Elequar and I am Jagaphant" Jagaphant answered.

"So, what is Crocapus' brothers name?"

"Octadile. Bumblepine is Porcubee's brother."

"Oh! everyone here has a brother. Well, everyone except me" Timmy said sadly.

"Yeah, but you have a magical treasure hunt though" Jagaphant answered, he didn't want his friend sad. Timmy had been nice to him and he talked as much as he like to himself.

"Yeah, I know. Shall we look at the clue together?" Timmy said instantly cheering up again.

" yes let's"

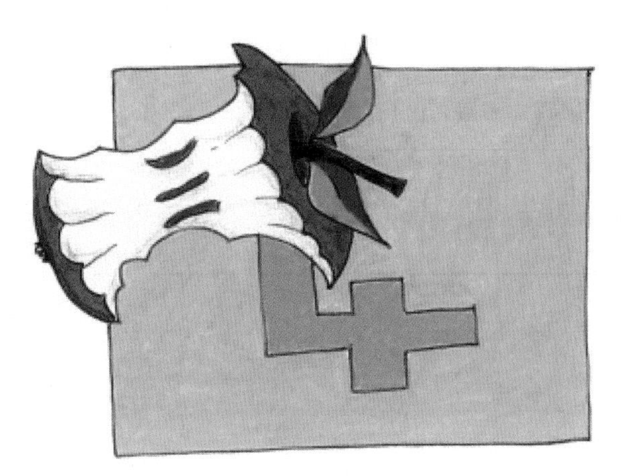

Timmy opened the envelope with Jagaphant looking over his shoulder, together they read out

"Clue number 4

To find clue number 5
Look to watch a fish dive!
Walk 3 steps forward,
From the edge of the sea
Then look up, look down,
For the count 1, 2, 3."

"I have to find the sea Jagaphant, all the other clues have been about the land, this is about the sea" Timmy was once again rambling away whilst bouncing up and down.

"Yeah, that does sound like fun" Jagaphant answered sadly

"Why do you sound sad Jagaphant?" Timmy asked.

"Well, you have to go now, and I like you, you are my friend, you talk a lot like I do. I liked it when you were here talking to me, but I know you got to go and finish your treasure hunt now."

"Do you want to come too Jagaphant?" Timmy asked, he really wanted him to come, especially as none of the others had wanted to.

"Really? You would let me come with you to the sea to find the next clue?" Jagaphant was clearly surprised.

"Of course! We can have so much fun and we can talk and talk as much as we like" Timmy said getting more and more excited and talking faster and faster.

"Whoop" Jagaphant fist pumped "let's go hunt."

And off the pair went to find where the sea was. As they walked, they talked, sometimes at the same time but both were happy.

"Look Jagaphant there it is, there is the sea and look there is a fish diving too" Timmy pointed out as they came across the water's edge, bouncing up and down with excitement.

"Read the clue again Timmy, what does it say? We need to make sure we do it right cos we don't want to miss the clue" Jagaphant was now also bouncing up and down with excitement.

"Walk 3 steps forward from the edge of the sea
Then look up look down for the count of 1, 2,3"

“Hey that’s Bumblepine over there, I bet he will have the next clue”

The pair ran over to Bumblepine.

“Hello Timmy, Hello Jagaphant, I didn’t expect to see you Jagaphant” Bumblepine said

“Well he was sad and so I asked him if he wanted to come and we have had lots of fun” Timmy said, at the same time Jagaphant said “well I was sad and Timmy asked me if I wanted to go with him and we had lots of fun”

The pair looked at each other and laughed.

“I can see you did and are still having lots of fun” Bumblepine laughed along with them. “Right then onto this clue, what have you got to do now?”

“Look up and look down for the count of 1, 2, 3” both answered together, resulting in another fit of giggles.

"Right then you two, how about I count and you two can do the looking up and looking down" Bumblepine interrupted their giggles with the hope of getting back on track.

"Yes" Timmy said

"Ok" Jagaphant said.

Both looked up and looked down.

"One!"

They looked up and down again.

"Two!"

They looked up and down a final time,

"Three!" said Bumblepine, as he said the word an envelope fell to the purple sand in front of them. This one said 'number 5' on the front.

"Who is going to open it?" Bumblepine asked,

"You do it" both replied, again this resulted in another fit of giggles.

"How about I read it out" Bumblepine said loudly to be heard over the giggles.

"Yes please" they both said.

Bumblepine was glad for something to look at beside the two overly excited ones in front of him because all their bouncing was making him feel seasick.

"X marks the spot

To find your final treasures place
I want you to put a smile on a face.

So, find the cave,
Where the grumpy one does live
And he has the treasure,
For you to give.

But to get the treasure
From him to you,
Make him smile,
Is what you must do".

Bumblepine looked over the top of the clue at the two faces in front of him "well there you have your final clue, I must admit I am surprised that is where your treasure is, with the grumpy one also known as Octadile."

"Octadile, but why, why do we have to go to him, he is always mean and grumpy" Jagaphant whined,

"But we won't get the treasure if we don't go" Timmy pleaded.

"I will come some of the way, but not all of it because Octadile scares me" Jagaphant answered

"What about you Bumblepine? Are you coming too?" Timmy asked as Bumblepine passed him the clue,

"No thank you Timmy, I am not a fan of his grumpiness, I am going to go now" and ***poof*** Bumblepine had disappeared.

The two set off, for once not chattering away, both were lost in their own thoughts.

A little while later.

"Stop Timmy" Jagaphant said "I'm sorry I don't want to go any further, but just keep going to the ***4th tree***, and then go towards the bush with the ***rainbow***

flowers on, you will know which one I mean when you see it" as Jagaphant was talking he was slowly retreating away from Timmy "bye Timmy. Thank-You for being my friend, and good luck" and then ***poof*** Jagaphant disappeared.

"Jeez, what is with them all just ***poofing*** off into nowhere" Timmy wondered out loud.

He carried on walking, the whole time talking to himself, (well come on just because there was no body to listen to him, didn't mean he didn't have anything to say)

"Everyone says Octadile is a grumpy, but no one has said WHY he is grumpy. My Mum says no one is born grumpy and there will be a reason somewhere you just have to find it".

Timmy had arrived at the first tree.

Jagaphant said the ***4th tree*** so Timmy carried on.

"My Mum said my Dad is always a grump when he is tired, but that doesn't make sense because if Octadile was tired he could just go to sleep" Timmy was once again talking to himself.

"Hi Timmy"

"Oh! hello Elequar"

"Bumblepine told me he gave you your final clue and that you have to find Octadile, you do remember what I told you about him not being a very nice chap don't you?"

"Yes Elequar, I remember. Everyone keeps telling me he is not nice, or he is grumpy, but no one has told me why. Do YOU know why he is that way Elequar?"

"I don't care to know; I have no time for people who aren't nice!"

"Well, I am going to ask him when I find him, do you want to come too?"

"No thank you, just keep going now to the ***3rd tree***, then look for the bush with the ***rainbow flowers*** on it, then when you get to that bush look for the ***blue banana tree***. Please don't be too sad if you don't get your treasure Timmy. Goodbye" and ***poof*** Elequar was gone.

"Treasure? Oh yeah, I kind of forgot about that, I was too busy thinking about Octadile and why he is grumpy. My Mum says" Timmy carried on towards the ***2nd tree***.

"That sometimes Dad gets a bit grumpy when he is hungry. But that doesn't make sense either because if Octadile was hungry he could just get some food. Because this magical island has lots of yummy things to eat" Timmy arrived at the ***2nd tree***.

"Hello again Timmy"

"Oh! hello Porcubee. Do you want to come with me to ask Octadile why he is grumpy?" Timmy asked,

"Why on earth would I want to do that?" Porcubee looked very confused.

"Everyone keeps telling me that Octadile is mean or not nice or grumpy, but no one has told me why. Do YOU know why?"

"Nope. Not my problem. I keep away from grumpy creatures if I can. I don't think you will manage to make him smile though, so you may not get your treasure. But carry on now to the ***2nd tree***, then find the bush with my

Dads favourite ***rainbow flowers*** on, then find the ***blue banana tree*** and then look out for ***the purple sandcastle***. Bye Timmy and good luck" and ***poof*** he too disappeared.

Timmy carried on to the ***3rd tree***.

"Oh yeah! the treasure I had forgotten about that again; I can't stop thinking about why Octadile is the way he is. I really want to know. So even if I don't make him smile, I still want to ask him."

"Hey Timmy. You ok? Sorry I left you before I was really freaked out, I still am, but I just wanted to make sure you were ok,"

"Hey Jagaphant, it's ok, but don't you ever wonder why Octadile is the way he is. My mum said there is always a reason for someone being mean or grumpy?"

"Well, I guess I never really thought about it to be honest. He just scares me,"

"Well, I can't stop thinking about it and I am going to ask him. Do you want to come too?" Timmy hoped Jagaphant would say yes because he had been kind of lonely on his own.

"No thank you Timmy, I am too scared of him. But just go to the ***last tree*** now then to the bush with the ***rainbow flowers***, then to the ***blue banana tree***, then to the ***purple sandcastle*** and then to the ***ice cream rock***"

"Ice cream rock?" Timmy asked,

"Yeah" Jagaphant chuckled "it's very cool and you can't miss it!"

Bye Jagaphant" Timmy said as he started making his way towards the last tree.

"My Mum says when I am under the weather, I get grumpy. I don't know what she means by under the weather because it doesn't make sense to me, but I know when I was poorly last time, I felt really miserable and sad and grumpy, so maybe Octadile doesn't feel well" Timmy pondered as he arrived at the ***last tree***.

"Now I have to go to the bush with the ***rainbow flowers*** that Porcubee's Dad likes" Timmy said looking around to see which direction he needed to go next.

"Yes, you do, then from there go to the ***blue banana tree***, then to the ***purple sandcastle***, then to ***the ice cream rock***. Then you will see the cave, it has a big '***X***' painted on the outside that Octadile put there. My brother is not going to smile Timmy" Crocapus said shaking his head.

"But why Crocapus, why is your brother so grumpy? Has he always been grumpy? Because my Mum says there is always a reason for someone being grumpy or for being mean, you just have to find out what it is."

"No, he hasn't always been grumpy, we used to all have lots of fun together, but one day he stopped smiling but I don't know why he is the way he is."

"Have you ever asked him?"

"No actually I haven't, he just seems to get more and more grumpy as time goes on."

"Well, I am going to ask him, and NOT because I want the treasure but because I think it's sad that no one knows. Goodbye Crocapus" Timmy said as he stomped away. He was very cross with Crocapus and all the others for not wanting to know what was wrong with Octadile.

"My mum says Old Man Miles, whoops I am not supposed to call him that My Mum says it's rude, I am supposed to call him Mr. Miles. Anyway, my Mum said Mr. Miles down the road is sad because he is lonely and that sometimes makes him a bit grumpy. I bet Octadile is lonely too, especially if no one goes to see him!"

Timmy rambled on as he passed the bush with the ***rainbow flowers*** that Porcubee's Dad likes so much. The bush was very cool. The flowers were shaped like little rainbows. Timmy thought his mum would love them too.

Timmy carried on to the ***blue banana tree*** as he had been instructed.

When he arrived at the ***blue banana tree*** Timmy took a quick rest, treasure hunting was hard work you know. Timmy plucked one of the blue bananas from the tree. "I think Octadile could be lonely, I have been lonely when I have been on my own, oh this banana is blue inside too, but it doesn't taste like any banana I have ever eaten before" Timmy said talking round a mouthful of the blue banana that didn't taste like a banana at all.

"That is because you have never been to this magical island before Timmy" Bumblepine laughed

"Hello Bumblepine, have you come to tell me what a grump Octadile is and that I won't get him to smile, just like all the others have? Because it doesn't matter. I am still going to find him, and I am going to ask him why he is so grumpy. Because I think it is sad, I bet he is lonely like old man Miles, I mean Mr. Miles down the road, because it is NOT like any of you visit him" Timmy stomped off to find the ***purple sandcastle*** before Bumblepine had chance to answer.

Timmy was really cross with all of them, even though they were his new friends. They all kept saying Octadile was grumpy and mean but how can they not see that they were being mean to him too.

Timmy carried on stomping and talking as he passed the very cool ***purple sandcastle***. It was a sandcastle but a real castle too. It had turrets and a drawbridge and even a moat and it was huge.

Timmy was STILL stomping and STILL cross and STILL talking to himself when he reached the ***ice cream rock***.

Timmy really wished they had something like this at home. It was shaped like an ice cream cone that you would get from the ice cream man. The sauce they dribble on the top were the slides down it. And the cone was a climbing area. Yes, Timmy really wished they had one of those back home, but he was still to cross at the others to stop and try it out.

He carried on stomping and talking to himself all the way to the cave with the big *'X'* painted on the side that Octadile had done.

While Timmy had been stomping and talking to himself and being cross with the others, he hadn't realised the others had joined him and had been following him, so when he turned around and saw all his new friends he was surprised.

Crocapus, Elequar, Porcubee, Jagaphant and Bumblepine were all there.

"Don't tell me, I know that Octadile is grumpy and I shouldn't go in" Timmy shouted at them. His mum would no doubt not be pleased with him for shouting and being rude but he couldn't help it.

"Well actually" said Crocapus first,

"The thing is" Elequar tried,

"I thought maybe" said Porcubee,

"I think that" Jagaphant stammered,

"Maybe you are right" finished Bumblepine.

They all started talking over one another no one was listening as everyone was talking all at the same time.

Then there was a really LOUD whistle and everyone stopped and turned to the source of the whistle.

"What are you ALL doing here?" Said Octadile "I knew Timmy would show up at some point because HE wants his treasure but why are you here oh brother dear? And you Elequar and Bumblepine, what brings you to this part of the island? My part of the island I might add. And you young Jagaphant and Porcubee what are you doing here. Come to make fun of the grumpy one, have you?" Octadile glared at them all one by one, he did not look or sound happy to see any of them.

They all looked away apart from Timmy who stepped forward with his hand out ready to shake his, well he would say hand, but he didn't have hands as such.

"Mr. Octadile" Timmy started

"No Mr. Just Octadile if you please"

"Sorry Octadile. I came because……." Timmy started again,

"Yes, I know why YOU came; YOU came because YOU want YOUR treasure, YOU think YOU can make ME smile, we'll go ahead and try, but it WILL NOT WORK" no, he was definitely not happy to see them.

"Octadile" Timmy started again stepping closer,

"I did come to begin with for my treasure. Because the final clue says:

Find the cave,
Where the grumpy one does live
And he has the treasure,
For you to give

But to get the treasure
From him to you
Make him smile,
Is what you must do.

"And so yeah, I started out to come here and try and get you to smile and then get my treasure,"

"Like. I. Said. GET. ON. WITH. IT." Octadile was clearly losing his patience and Timmy could see why the others called him grumpy,

"But then I changed my mind Octadile" Timmy bravely carried on as though Octadile hadn't spoken at all "I changed my mind and now I am NOT here about the treasure. Yes, I was excited to do the treasure hunt and even when I started towards here after Bumblepine gave me the final clue I was thinking about the treasure. But then, as I walked past the ***four trees***, and as I passed by the bush with the very cool ***rainbow flowers***, and the ***blue banana tree*** where the bananas are blue but don't actually taste like bananas, and the ***purple sandcastle*** and the ***ice cream rock*** which looks so very cool and I really wish we had one at home, I stopped thinking about the treasure Octadile, because all I could think about was YOU!"

"Mmmmmmmmmmmmmeeeeeeeeeeeeeee?" Octadile sort of screeched and stammered "why me? No one ever thinks about ME. No one ever visits ME or wants to see ME. So why would YOU.BE. THINKING. ABOUT. ME?" Octadile had gotten louder and louder until he was shouting the final words.

"Because all my new friends were really nice to me, and all they are telling me was that you were a grump, or you were not nice, or you were rude or mean and scary. But Octadile not one of my new friends who I am still quite cross with, although not as cross as I was because they are here after all, anyway not one of them knew WHY you were so grumpy. And my Mum says that no one is just grumpy and mean there is always a reason you just need to find that reason.

"My Mum says my Dad gets grumpy when he is hungry or tired, but I don't think that is why you are grumpy. Because if you were tired you could sleep. If you were hungry you could eat. My Mum says I get grumpy when I am under the weather, but I don't really know what that means, but I do know I am sad and miserable and grumpy when I don't feel very well. So, I thought that might be a reason, but then surely your brother would know if you weren't very well. And then my Mum says that Mr. Miles, well I usually call him Old Man Miles, but I am trying not to because my Mum said it's rude,"

Octadile was looking at Timmy like something he had never seen before. Even Jagaphant didn't seem to talk quite as much without stopping. Unless he did, but he was used to Jagaphant.

"Mr. Miles?" Octadile nervously asked,

"Mr. Miles lives down the road from me, and sometimes he is really grumpy and mean, but my Mum says that it is because he is sad and lonely. Because his wife died, and his dog ran away. So really, he isn't grumpy he is just sad. But that is why I was thinking about you. Why are you grumpy Octadile? Are you sad? Are you tired? Are you hungry? Are you not feeling well? Are you lonely?" Timmy knelt in the purple sand in front of Octadile.

"You would give up your treasure to find out why I am grumpy?" Octadile asked in a very quiet voice,

"Yes. My Mum says treasures and gifts come in all sorts of shapes and sizes.

I didn't really get what she meant, so she said that some of the best treasures can't be held in your hand. This confused even more. But I think I get it now Octadile. Will you tell me what makes you grumpy please Octadile?

"Yes! please tell us" Crocapus said,

"I would like to know too" Elequar added,

"And me" said Porcubee,

"Me also" said Bumblepine.

"I would like to know too, cos you scare. I don't know if I will stop fearing you by knowing, but Timmy kept asking us and none of us knew. So please Octadile will you tell us." Octadile couldn't help but smile a little on the inside, that was the Jagaphant he remembered, why use one or three words when you can use a whole load of them.

Octadile looked at them all one by one. Then turned to look just at Timmy and said in a small voice. "I have lost my favourite book. And that made me sad. Then because I was sad, I was a bit grumpy. Now no one wants to talk to me or visit me, then you Timmy come along and are willing to give up your treasure because YOU wanted to know why I was grumpy." Octadile was clearly confused,

"No one ever asked. No one ever cared to know. So, I didn't want to tell them. This made me sadder and grumpier. Then they didn't want to see me, so I became lonely and even more sad and grumpy" Octadile felt a little bit ashamed and didn't know who to look at anymore and so he just looked at the floor.

"Octadile" Jagaphant said bravely "I have lots and lots of books at home would you like one of those instead?"

"But you are scared of me, you said so yourself, why would you want to give me one of your books?"

"You don't seem quite so scary now you just seem sad, I don't like being sad and I don't like my friends being sad, so if I can help, I want to. I was sad when Timmy was going on his treasure hunt without me, so Timmy asked me if I wanted to go with him, and that made me happy. I would like to give you one of my books if that would make you happy" Jagaphant said.

"Thank you Jagaphant I would like that a lot."

"Octadile I am sorry. I should have asked you what was wrong when you first became sad. Thank you, Timmy, for wanting to know why our friend was sad. Octadile? Why was that book your favourite one?" Bumblepine asked.

"It had some really special pictures in it" Octadile answered, still not quite looking at anyone but not quite looking at the floor either.

"I have some very cool pictures at my house if you would like some of them, or I could draw you some new ones" Porcubee said hopefully.

"That would be nice thank you Porcubee" Octadile was starting to sound a lot less sad.

"Was there anything else about your favourite book that made it so special Octadile?" asked Elequar,

"I don't want to tell you cos you will laugh and think I am stupid" Octadile was back to sounding sad again.

"No one will laugh. I pinkie promise Octadile. And no-one thinks you are stupid." Timmy said turning and looking at the others "will you?" he demanded,

"No" they all said.

"There were no words in it. I don't like the words cos the letters get all mixed up. It's like they are dancing on the page. And it means I can't read them. But my book had lots of pictures so I could just make up my own stories!"

"Octadile, I am so sorry I didn't know. Dad is the same, so am I. You know those glasses I wear when I am reading, well they are magic glasses and Dad has some too. They stop the letters dancing" Crocapus said coming forward "how about you and I go and talk to Dad?"

"I didn't know it was like that for you and Dad too. I always thought I was stupid, or you would laugh at me" Octadile looked at Crocapus "I am NOT stupid, I'm not."

"No Octadile. You are NOT stupid. You are a very clever brother. You just need some extra help is all, and the magic glasses will do that."

Octadile looked around at his old friends who were all smiling, and his new friend Timmy who was once again bouncing up and down, and for the first time since he lost his favourite book, Octadile smiled.

"Hey, he is smiling, Octadile is smiling, look! does that mean Timmy will get his treasure after all?" Asked Jagaphant excitedly

"Oh yes he is, it's been a long time since we saw that" said Elequar.

"It has most certainly has been a while," said Bumblepine.

"Timmy should get his treasure then really," said Porcubee.

"What do you think Timmy, would you like your treasure?" Octadile asked

Timmy who was once again bouncing.

"Yes please! I would love my treasure!" Timmy replied

"Here you go Timmy,

Close your eyes,
Then count to 3
Then collect your treasure,
But what will it be?"

Octadile said.

Timmy closed his eyes,

"One, two, three"

When he opened his eyes again, he was back at home in his room, in bed.

There next to him was hie treasure and a little note that said:

The treasure you found,
After a magical time,
Having made some new friends,
And a partner in crime.

You saw magical things,
And places as well,
Will you go back?
Well, who can tell.

But even if you don't,
You can remember it all,
Just open your treasure
To relive and recall.

A book is your treasure,
But don't look yet,
Because a memory is always
The best treasure to get.

So, now open the book
To remember the magical land,
With its rainbow flowers
And its purple sand.

Remember your new friends,
We won't ever be too far,
Love Crocapus, Octadile, Bumblepine

Porcubee, Jagaphant and Elequar.

Timmy excitedly opened the book. There in front of him he saw page after page reminding him of the creatures, he met that became his new friends and the things of amazement he saw too.

When Timmy got to the end it was a bit different to the ending of Timmy's adventure. The treasure came with a note that read:

Your wish for a brother
Will soon come true,
Your mum has exciting,
News just for you.

Now you don't have,
To wish for a brother,
Your mum will give you,
One after another.

You may even get a sister,
That will be cool too,
You will always be their hero,
And they will look up to you.

So, a new name you will have,
A big brother you will be,
You can help feed them all,
And bounce them upon your knee.

Tell them your story,
Show them your magical book,
You never know one day,
They may come for a look.

Just as Timmy got to the end of the note in the book his Mum shouted, "Timmy can you come down please, Dad and I have some very exciting news to share with you".

THE END

Epilogue

TO START YOUR ADVENTURE
JUST OPEN YOUR BOOK
TURN THE FIRST PAGE
AND TAKE A LOOK

WHERE WILL IT TAKE YOU?
WHERE WILL YOU BE?
DINOSAURS OR TREASURES?
I CAN'T WAIT TO SEE.

Where will Timmy's next adventure take him?

About the Author

I am a married lady, on the higher side of 45, I have lived in Nottingham England (Robin Hood Land) all my life apart from a few years where I moved to the posh Harrogate, I am not posh and it didn't work.

I am a bit like Henry V111 but instead of "divorced beheaded died" I have Alcoholic, Psycho and died. So I am a bit of a serial name changer, I am married to hubby number 4 but I know this time I have found my soul mate. He is the fish to my chips, the salt to my vinegar, the yin to my yang. My Dude is my life.

I have an older sister and an older brother plus an array of nieces and nephews, some blood some adopted, but I love them all.

I currently work in a betting shop which whilst I love it can sometimes be stressful.

I am Big, I am Inked, My hair colour changes like the weather (which in England can be four seasons in a day) and I am in your face loud. I don't do egg shells and I don't do cotton wool.

I am very much the kind of person who is happy in herself and if someone doesn't like me they can turn right around and find the door they came through.

I have worked hard and shed many tears to be happy in my own skin.

I am nothing special, I have always liked words and enjoyed playing with them, sometimes in the form of a poem others in the form of a story. It was only during the pandemic of 2020 when the whole of the UK was under strict lockdown that I found my love once again for words and writing.

I sat one day and started writing.

It took me on a journey of heartache, pain, tears, and self-discovery. I never in all my wildest dreams expected it to turn out as detailed as it is.

But that is the thing with pain you don't realise how bad it is until you start to explore it.

This very real very true account of not only being the victim (I hate that word so much) of domestic violence but a survivor (much better word), It isn't pretty, it isn't a fairy tale. It is harrowing, dark and upsetting.

It has taken me a long and painful journey to be at the point in life where I can discuss what happened to me, and some of that is through this book. I revealed things in there for my readers I have never told anyone before so writing it and sharing it wasn't easy.

But if I can reach just ONE person, and help them then I know all my pain is worth it.

Domestic violence is never OK, someone saying they are sorry does not excuse them.

Abuse takes form in so many different forms, it can be emotional or physical. It can be sexual.

Never is it ok for one person to be abused in anyway by someone they love. Not a woman, not a man not a child.

You can connect with me on:

- https://www.facebook.com/mandyswiftson
- https://www.facebook.com/lanasportraits

Printed in Great Britain
by Amazon